TEMPEST OF ANGELS

Also by R. D. G. Lover

Angels' Compass
Tempest of Angels
Inheriting Armageddon

The Tides of Amelia Island
The Storm & the Sea
Rose Tide & Rust

the wisteria collection
wisteria, vol. I

Coloring Books
The Amelia Island Coloring Book

TEMPEST OF ANGELS

AN ANGELS' COMPASS SHORT STORY

R. D. G. LOVER

4pocalypse Arts

4pocalypse Arts

For those who weather the storms.

For our struggle is not against flesh and blood, but against the rulers, against the authorities, against the powers of this dark world and against the spiritual forces of evil in the heavenly realms.

Ephesians 6:12 (NIV)

AUTHOR'S NOTE

I have found that as time goes on, I care less about what people think and more about doing the things I love. I recently found a printed copy of *Tempest of Angels* when I was unpacking my office supplies in my new house. I'd forgotten I'd even printed it at all. That's when it hit me: I write these books for me. The joy I felt holding the book was incredible. There it was, the physical manifestation of my love and over a decade of dedication to the craft. My heart bursts at the seams when I hold my stories.

So here's another small piece of my heart.

In 2021, I wrote this short story as a casual introduction to my characters and window into their world. I started posting it online, but I never quite finished posting it anywhere. Thus, this story has lived in my Scrivener files for the last five years.

I wanted this story to be a hook for the series, but as time went on and I got more beta readers, it became clear to me that the story of Angels' Compass may be too large to condense down into a tiny seventy-page book.

Having already published *Inheriting Armageddon*, I think now is the right time to release this story. *Tempest of Angels* can be read before or after *Inheriting Armageddon*, but *Inheriting Armageddon* will give you better grounding in the world of Angels' Compass. If you read *Tempest of Angels* after *Inheriting Armageddon*, it is a short and sweet return to these characters. If you read *Tempest of Angels* first, just know that a whole world is waiting for you in the next book.

As stated in the author's note of *Inheriting Armageddon:* Any use of angels and demons and the like in this book is purely fictitious and my own creative twist; it is not meant to be a serious or accurate portrayal of these matters. This book also contains adult themes such as violence, swearing, brief sexual content, assassin activities, and use of drugs, alcohol, and weapons.

GLOSSARY

— HIERARCHY (IN ORDER OF POWER) —

Archangels – the highest ranking angel to walk the Earth, they oversee human affairs; they are placed on Earth every few hundred years to chart humanity's progress; they can compel humans to choose to be virtuous rather than sinful; they represent the Eight Virtues: Joy, Humility, Liberality, Patience, Diligence, Chastity, Abstinence, and Kindness

Archangel Heirs – the children of two Archangels

Nephilim – the children of one Archangel and one human; human women often die giving birth to the children of male Archangels

Halfbreed – children conceived by an angel and a demon, delivered by an angel (Angelborne) or demon (Demonborne)

Sentinels – guardian angels who take the angelic form that is the lower half of a land-dwelling creature (Landborne) or a sea-dwelling creature (Seaborne); (slang: *nymph* {for Landborne Sentinels} and *siren* {for Seaborne Sentinels})

Saints – humans who have been ordained by Archangels or the Church for a holy purpose

— IMPORTANT TERMS —

Unseen Wars – invisible battles between angels and demons that happen on Earth, during day-to-day life, especially during storms or other natural disasters

Marks – protections cast by angels, much like spells or enchantments; some examples are Binding Marks, which suppress the affected's power, and Cloaking Marks, which hide one's true nature from being detected

Archangel Tattoo – a tattoo which Marks the ranks of Archangel, Archangel Heir, Nephilim, or Halfbreed

North Academy – an advanced high school academy for those with angelic blood, founded by Valentine North

RUST – blacklisted assassin organization, banned from killing besides after dark; the assassins employed here exclusively wear black; founded by Cephan, located within the Abyss

The Mediating Grounds – the plane between Heaven and Earth; this is where angels and demons alike come to report to God's Spokesperson

— CHARACTERS (BY APPEARANCE) —

Venatrix Canes – Archangel Heir, youngest Canes sibling

Erin Canes – Archangel Heir, middle Canes sibling

Caeleb Canes – Archangel Heir, oldest Canes sibling

Corvun Khlyde – Nephilim, firstborn son of Michael and Valkyrie

Cynthia Khlyde – Nephilim, daughter of Michael and Valkyrie

Michael Khlyde – Archangel, the Virtue of Liberality, father of Corvun and Cynthia

Ophiah Jude – Angelborne Halfbreed, twin to Orion

Orion Jude – Angelborne Halfbreed, twin to Ophiah

Casper North – Archangel Heir, son of Valentine and Gabrielle

Cassie North – Archangel Heir, firstborn daughter of Valentine and Gabrielle

Jayren Omans – Seaborne Sentinel

Krista Martin – Saint decadency, girlfriend of Caeleb

Shanvi Sinclair – Landborne Sentinel, girlfriend of Erin

Mila Kardon – Prophetess

Kadhi Rajesh – Landborne Sentinel, boyfriend of Cassie

Joshuah Braidensen – Landborne Sentinel

Valentine North – Archangel, the Virtue of Joy, father of Cassie and Casper, headmaster of North Academy

Gabrielle North – Archangel, the Virtue of Humility, mother of Cassie and Casper

Dr. Ralph Bennett – Archangel, the Virtue of Diligence

ANGELS

a poem

Don't you know
that angels dance in storms
with footsteps across ponds and
stampedes across the oceans?

Do you hear the warhorses
in the thunder and see
the glint of holy steel
cut across the sky?

These are the unseen wars,
the supernatural forces who battle
in the heat of the storm and the
rage of the wind;
where Heaven and Hell
clash across the clouds,
where they meet in the middle
to wage a war for our souls
which both intend to win.

r. d. g. lover

I

VENATRIX CANES

The bathroom smelled like skunk.

Venatrix stood there, rubbing her eyes with cold water, glancing up every now and then to stare at her murky reflection through the condensation on the mirror. She was a blotchy, bleary mess of black hair and pale skin, like the blurred sight of a heap of chess pawns. She'd always thought smoking weed would make you dumber, funnier, stupid even. But all she felt was vertigo and her dinner making its way back up her throat.

Bloodshot blue eyes—she couldn't pull it off like her brothers, who had given her the joint. Caeleb and Erin looked cool when they were high, laid back, uncaring. The girls laughed at her brothers more. Venatrix wondered if that's why she'd really done it—if she'd smoked to be the star of all the attention, to look cool and be liked. She wondered if maybe it was just a stunt not to get kicked out of the party her brothers threw. She didn't want to go, but she didn't want to be left out.

She didn't really have anywhere else to go, either.

Someone knocked on the door.

Venatrix clutched her towel and cracked it open.

It was Corvun. He was stoned, too. "Are you okay?" His voice was gravelly.

Venatrix nodded. "Had enough of the party."

Corvun gave her a small, rare smile.

It was true. She'd retreated upstairs, washed her body in hopes to drench the smell, planned to go to bed and fake waking up when her parents crashed the party the next morning. She'd found the company of the soap dispenser way more soothing; the mosaic, mix-match of the iridescent glass bottle showed her different versions of her face, different people she could be. She *wanted* to be independent—of her brothers, of the boys they set her up with, of the reputation she had of getting sky-high and dancing on tables with Corvun.

"I hate being high," she told Corvun. Tears dotted her eyelashes.

"Do you want to go sit on the roof?"

Venatrix nodded.

"Meet you there in five?" he asked.

She nodded again.

. . . .

Venatrix's hair was still wet when she ducked out her bedroom window to climb the roof. She found Corvun there already, his neck craned towards the silhouette of twisting live oak branches and dripping Spanish moss. The distant city illuminated the horizon, but darkness hung over the house. Venatrix found a perch beside her best friend and pulled her damp hair over her shoulder. In the humid-cool night, it made her feel even more sticky. Venatrix squirmed, picked her plastered-on shirt from under her armpits.

The bumping music from downstairs could be heard from where they sat.

Corvun laid back and stretched his long legs. "Stargazin' is way cooler than that shitshow downstairs," he said.

"You're just saying that to make me feel better." She laid beside him. The stars blinked overhead, like a mini-city in the sky. She wondered if it was Heaven.

"Your brothers were tryin' to hook me up with one of the girls," Corvun confided.

"Welcome to my world."

"Have you ever—"

"I know you're not asking me this," Venatrix interrupted.

Corvun leaned on his elbow and looked at her. "—done it?"

Venatrix shoved him, and he laughed.

It was silent for a moment.

"You first."

"No," Corvun said. "I don't know, it just seems like somethin' you should save for someone important to you."

"Agreed." She didn't want to tell him about the boys she'd kissed while sitting on their laps, about the peer pressure she'd given in to or the names that held those dark secrets above her. Corvun had always been better at saying no and walking away.

"If you ever need me to beat Caeleb or Erin up…"

Venatrix rolled her head to the side to look at him.

Corvun's eyes flashed across the sky above them. Dark freckles spotted his pale skin and bluish bags stained the skin beneath his brown eyes. It was clear he'd been losing sleep more and more as the days went on. Venatrix couldn't remember the last time his eyes didn't look tired.

"I know," Venatrix said. "Except, I think you're trying to make up excuses to do it these days."

Corvun laughed.

CORVUN KHLYDE

When the sky began to turn silver-blue and the stars resigned, Corvun and Venatrix climbed back through her bedroom window. Venatrix gave Corvun a tight hug around the neck, and he warily put his palms on her fragile back, the bones and ribs that read like braille under his fingers. She wasn't made to fit in to any whim or fad her brothers were; bending her into those shapes would break her. She was her own spirit, her own piece of art. Corvun knew she couldn't see it, but he could.

Corvun left her on the edge of her bed and pulled her door shut. Her parents weren't supposed to be home for another few hours.

Downstairs, the party was wilting. Bottles of champagne and aged wine sat empty on the counter like glass tombstones, embellished in curling letters of their sugary promises. *How wasted can you get on wine?* Corvun wondered. Boys and girls from his class lounged across the Canes's furniture, drool seeping from their lips, hiccuping the sour-sweet smell of the alcohol. A few joints were scattered like weeds across the house. Three on the stove. One on the side table with a compass coaster and a ring of paling water beside it.

Corvun stared at the compass design. It was etched in a square, sandy-stone material, leaving the compass a scar-white. *Like on skin,* Corvun thought. *That's what the brand will look like on my skin.*

Everyone knew that the compass was a symbol closely associated with the assassin organization, RUST. It was a brand burned on the right wrist, reminiscent of a knife up a sleeve. Only, the brand was to mark the assassins as the weapons themselves. Corvun, since turning twelve, had known his life was promised to the organization. Corvun tried his best to understand it the way his father, Michael, had explained it: Michael was in RUST for several years, his first real job after moving to the Jacksonville area. He didn't expect to meet anyone—much less fall in love with a woman with no ties to RUST. Michael told Corvun that the only way the leader agreed to let him walk free of the organization, to marry the woman he loved, was to promise his firstborn to RUST at the age of nineteen.

Corvun was just caught in the crossfire.

. . . . .

Corvun walked home. After all, his house was just down the street from Venatrix's. The wind rustled through the trees as he jogged up the small steps to the front door. He crouched by the flowerbed just to the right of the threshold, grabbing for the fake stone there and the spare key it hid inside.

The door swung open before he could find it.

Cynthia, his younger sister, stood with her hair in a towel and heat-splotched hands on her hips. Her face was red, and she smelled like waterlily soap and peppermint toothpaste. "Do you have any idea how much trouble you're about to be in?" she asked.

Corvun sighed, stood, and pushed his way past his sister.

Inside, his father and his stepmother bustled around the kitchen. The toaster gave a metallic *pop* as the smell of toast drifted through the house. Corvun considered he must still smell like the party, so he did his best to stand still when his parents fixed glares on him.

Michael side-stepped the kitchen counter and stalked to him. "What have I told you about parties on weekdays?"

Corvun breathed in, held it, closed his eyes to keep his father from seeing them roll. "Vena asked me to go. I didn't want to leave her—"

"Don't come up with some chivalrous excuse. Miss Canes has her own free will. She could come stay here if she didn't like the parties," Michael snapped.

The idea made Corvun think. The parties that the Canes brothers threw were not under-the-radar. The school knew; the parents knew. The cops knew too, but there was too much other serious trouble in the city to tend to. Besides, risking their cops to dismantle a party in the dead of night only posed more of a danger. Night was when the RUST assassins ran wild; teenage parties were the least of the cops' concerns. But his father was right—Venatrix didn't have to stay there. So why did she? *Does she really like the parties?* Corvun wondered.

In their silence, the TV babbled in the corner. The news flashed to the weather. A spaghetti model of the latest hurricane. The newscaster chipped in, "The tropical storm, now upgraded to a category one hurricane, has been named Helix. Landfall is expected by the end of the week."

Corvun glanced at the blue and green satellite image on the TV. He sighed, knowing exactly what it would mean to Caeleb and Erin, to the rest of their tight circle of friends. *Hurricane party.* Corvun could already feel his father's disapproval brewing. But one thing was for sure: If Venatrix got herself tied up in going, there was no way Corvun would let her go alone.

II

OPHIAH JUDE

Ophiah sat in the back of the classroom with her hands tangled in Casper's. The tight-knit carpet under their feet smelled like stale soap, and the glossy, flesh-colored desks were freezing to the touch. The lights above were sterile and bright. Ophiah felt every bit under a microscope, being watched by everyone. Cold sweat dripped down her sides, chilling the thin, collared shirt she wore over a tank top. Even Casper's hands didn't offer her warmth or comfort—they were cold and clammy, but they were the only hands that would hold hers.

She watched the classroom as Casper whispered in her ear.

The longer she tried to listen, the less it sounded like language. His voice took on an ancient quality about it, something like the sound of a whisper in a church, faraway, and much too holy for her.

Venatrix whisked into the classroom like she did every morning—a high and mighty strut with her nose in the air. She had no traces of the party from the night before on her. Ophiah had known it was happening; Casper had attended and begged her to come. She refused. Ophiah could care less for parties, especially if it involved the Canes siblings. Casper liked to hang out with Caeleb and Erin, but it made him a different person. He was more assertive and less sweet. He kissed her differently when the brothers were watching, and it made Ophiah uncomfortable.

Right on cue, Caeleb and Erin walked in—a saunter on Caeleb and a sulk on Erin. They weaved their way to the back of the classroom, like spiders closing in on the trap Casper had laid for Ophiah.

She pulled her hands away, feeling more and more cornered by the minute.

Caeleb sat, legs apart, in the chair ahead of Ophiah and Casper. Erin slouched in the chair just to their left, his eyes bloodshot. He was still high.

"I—have to go to the bathroom," Ophiah said. She stood.

Caeleb gazed up at her, his blue eyes dripping over her makeup, her hair, her necklace.

She just wished someone would see her for what was underneath it all.

Orion, her twin brother, slammed his books down on the seat to the right of them. His hands balled into fists, a subtle giveaway. Ophiah felt the intention from her twin; he wanted to strangle Caeleb, Erin, maybe even Casper. Anyone within reach it seemed.

"What's going on?" Ophiah whispered to him.

"Ask them," her twin hissed.

Caeleb grinned, his lower lip tucked into his teeth. He fixed his startling eyes right on Ophiah's. Then he flinched. A kick under the table. Casper snapped something under his breath, and Caeleb rolled his eyes and leaned back. "Helix hits this Friday," Caeleb said with a voice like river-smoothed stones. Dark, rolling. Words were natural music on his lips. His eyes flitted from Ophiah to Orion then back. "We know a house on Fletcher that has a backup generator. We'll have board games and drinks. Consider yourselves invited."

"We gotta get high to get in?" Orion bit the words.

Caeleb cocked an eyebrow at Orion. "If that's a deal breaker," he paused, "then no. Means more for us anyway."

Ophiah watched Orion. She let him make the decisions. He was better with his words. She expected him to turn the party down anyway, but his eyes wandered across the room and settled on their sister. Orion watched Venatrix throw her books down on her desk and crack them open. Ophiah gritted her teeth to keep from gaping. "Walk me to the bathroom?" she asked Orion tightly.

Orion heaved himself up and out of his seat as if he was an anchor on *her* ship. He seemed rooted to her, currents aside, and storms be damned. Ophiah couldn't understand the fascination anyone had with the Canes sister; she was impulsive and attention seeking. Ophiah followed fast on Orion's heels.

When they were outside the classroom, she stepped up to him. "Are you insane? A hurricane party? Do you have any idea how dangerous that is? Helix is already a category two!"

Orion's eyes glued to the door.

Ophiah shoved his chest. "Is this about Venatrix Canes?"

Orion shook his head, paling.

"What's your problem? Do you have a crush on her? You've never *talked* to her."

"She just doesn't seem like them. I just want to get to know her, you know?" Orion's brow furrowed. "She's *always* stuck at their parties."

"Stuck? She's the life of the party." Ophiah felt her skin getting hot. "She's a slut."

Orion's eyes locked on Ophiah. "You don't even know her."

"*You* don't even know her, Ri."

"Well I'm going," Orion said decidedly.

"Ten bucks says you won't even talk to her," Ophiah fumed.

Orion rolled his eyes and turned back into the classroom.

JAYREN OMANS

Jayren had a death wish. At least, that was sure as hell what it felt like. Jayren couldn't stop the bad decisions from rolling. He figured he'd roll with the punches, right to the grave. He sat next to Corvun at the lunch table at the very corner of the cafeteria, listening to Corvun go on about the hurricane party the Canes brothers were throwing that weekend. As far as the party went, Jayren had already made up his mind.

"They really put the 'canes in hurricanes, huh?" Jayren asked, deadpan. "Please don't tell me you're going. I thought you said you were gonna quit going to their parties."

"I did," Corvun mumbled.

Jayren had only been friends with Corvun for a few months, but the thought of losing him back to the cool kids made Jayren's stomach churn. Corvun was one of the best things that'd happened to him. For once he had a friend—a *real* friend. Jayren had almost considered telling Corvun about the voices he heard, too. "Can I come too, then?" *At least that way,* he thought, *I can stay friends with him.*

Corvun opened his mouth, closed his eyes, covered the lower half of his face with his hand. "I'm only goin' to make sure Vena doesn't get into trouble," he mumbled through his palm.

"You got the hots for her?"

"*No,*" Corvun insisted.

It was about the twentieth time Jayren had asked that question that period.

"She's like a sister to me," Corvun explained finally. "We grew up together."

Jayren nodded sympathetically, as if he understood. He hadn't been lucky enough to grow up with any friends at all. They usually found out he heard voices then called the friendship off around the same time.

Corvun continued, "She's smart. I don't know why she hangs out with them. She didn't used to like the parties, so I just—" Corvun huffed, "I don't understand why she still bothers with them at all. We used to *study* and go to dance practice."

"The only dance the North Academy has is ballet," Jayren said with a furrowed brow. It was more of a question than anything, but Corvun acted like Jayren hadn't said anything at all. "*Ballet*," Jayren said again, leaning closer to Corvun.

"Dude, I get it," Corvun snapped.

"Oh my god, you do ballet?"

Corvun glared at Jayren. "Do you have a problem with that?"

Jayren shook his head fervently. *God, idiot. You're gonna fuck it up with him.* He cleared his throat. "So you two are dance partners?" he asked casually. He'd caught the occasional rumor about it—they were dance partners at the Canes's parties, too. On tables. Half-naked. The thought made Jayren queasy.

Corvun looked away. "Used to be."

Jayren raised his eyebrows but didn't say anything. *Okay,* he thought. *Maybe those were lies.* He'd had plenty of lies passed around about him. It made him feel better that Corvun carried rumors, too.

"Will your parents let you go to the party?" Corvun asked, looking down at his tray of food for the first time since they sat down.

The question caught Jayren like a fishing hook to the stomach. It dragged his insides right out. He choked on a stutter, pinched his arm to get his shit together. It didn't work. *It's not working, it's not working.* He closed his eyes and fought the sickness rising into his throat like flood water in a storm drain. "Parents. Right. Yeah. Totally."

Corvun put his fork down slowly.

Jayren stood in a clatter. "I have to go."

"Where?" Corvun asked. He looked up at Jayren with big, round, brown eyes. He looked exactly like the type of guy a girl would consider a big softy, complete with the puppy-dog eyes and beauty marks.

Jayren cursed himself inwardly. "Bathroom," he mumbled.

He doesn't believe you.

Jayren left Corvun at the table and clawed at his own stomach.

He knows you're lying.

Liar.

Coward.

Jayren threw the bathroom door open with a *clang*, picked a stall, climbed up to the back of the toilet, and sat down on the water tank. He covered his ears, squeezed his eyes shut.

Then the voices came in thousands, swarming like locusts.

. . . .

Corvun stared after the hallway Jayren disappeared into. He sighed. He knew his mistake; the words slipped past his lips before he realized it, though. Corvun heard a share of gossip about Jayren, and he decided to turn a blind eye to all of it. He guessed he should've tread lightly on the topics he *had* heard about. Corvun stood, took both their trays in, then wandered to the bathroom.

He opened the door and stood in the silent, gray and white hall. One stall was closed.

Corvun breathed deep and stared at the ceiling. "Jay?"

"Stop! Stop!" Jayren's voice cracked through the locker room. "God, make them stop."

A hard fist twisted Corvun's gut. "Jay, it's Corvun."

Jayren sucked in a sob. "God, no. Leave me alone. Please."

Corvun took heavy steps over to Jayren's stall. "It's okay. I just came to talk."

"I live with my sister, okay? She'll never let me go!"

"Good thing I know how to sneak out," Corvun offered.

Jayren quieted. His feet hit the floor with two dry slaps. He shuffled over; the stall lock *clacked*. He opened the door. His green eyes were rubbed red and puffy. "You'd do that for me?"

"Why not?"

"Thanks man."

Corvun nodded. "Do you want to talk about…" he waved his hand, "you know."

Jayren shook his head.

"Well, I wanted to apologize."

"It's fine," Jayren said, sniffling. He brushed past Corvun. Corvun hesitated, then followed him out.

CORVUN KHLYDE

The first thing Corvun did when he got home was check for his parents' car and to make sure Cynthia was studying in her room. His heart rattled his chest. The plans he formulated jittered through his veins. The party was crossing a line. He knew it. That's why he would go, and that's why he wouldn't go unarmed.

Ever since the Third World War, weapons had been banned cross-country. When people had moved into the cities for protection, they were required to surrender their weapons, and within a few months of the ban and seizure, all of the weapons had been stolen by RUST. Crime skyrocketed. The government offered sweet-lipped lies of how they were working to recover the weapons and how the police force was sworn to protecting America's citizens. Most crimes happened at night, a grueling task even for a cop with a strong stomach. RUST assassins had Black Magic and the supernatural on their side. Whoever was on RUST's list, died. To make it worse, it was usually thoughtless, mindless, seemingly random killing of innocents for sport. Just the thought of it made Corvun sick.

The only remedy was the nine-millimeter Corvun knew his father had kept from his own time in RUST. Corvun figured, if he and the others were staying on an abandoned street in an abandoned town in the middle of a storm, the least he could do is have something to protect them all. He dug through Michael's nightstand, his step-mother's nightstand, their dresser, their closet. He was pulling Bibles from their bookshelf when Cynthia spoke.

"What are you doin'?"

Corvun's nerves turned electric. "Nothin'."

"That sure as hell doesn't look like *nothin'*."

Corvun reached into the shelf. He felt the grooved hilt of a gun.

"I'm goin' to tell dad," Cynthia said.

"No you won't," Corvun said. He lifted the heavy weapon, careful not to touch the trigger. He pulled it from the shelf and stared at the night-black pistol.

"Give me one good reason why I shouldn't tell him you're stealin' his *gun*."

"Because I'll let you come to the party if you promise not to say anythin'." He glanced at his sister. He knew she wanted to go to parties in the past; he also knew she had a crush on Jayren. It was his only leverage. "And Jay's goin' too."

She shifted on her heels, weighing her options. "And you won't tell dad if I drink?"

Corvun shook his head.

"Deal," Cynthia said.

"Deal." Corvun stuck the gun in the back of his pants. "Go pack a bag. We're leavin' in ten."

III

ORION JUDE

The old house smelled murky, like standing water, and it creaked in the wind. White silk sheets draped the furniture. The roar of the ocean rolled in through the foggy windows, and somewhere on the outside of the house, a clanking and clattering could be heard.

Orion glanced around the high ceilinged house, the tall, arched doorways, and the massive canvases hanging on the walls. Few other whispers filled the house; Orion listened in on the conversations.

"God, that was so awesome!" a nasally voice said. "I've never snuck out before. It's so fucking *liberating*. How did you learn how to do that?"

A mumble returned the chatter, too muted to hear.

A group of laughter walked up the stairs.

Orion turned around to see Caeleb, Erin, and Casper. Ophiah trailed behind them. Off to the corner, Corvun pulled some sheets free of the furniture, leaving dust clouds in their wake. A blond kid sulked next to him, and he waved his hand in theatrics as he thanked Corvun for letting him tag along. A younger girl—who was the spitting image of Corvun—flopped down onto the chair he'd just uncovered, and Corvun glared at her. *Siblings,* Orion could tell.

Orion pulled Erin aside. "Where's your sister?"

"Messing with the generator," Erin said.

"*Alone?*" Orion demanded. "It's nearly dark."

"Cassie's with her." Erin shrugged it off and side-stepped Orion to follow Caeleb into the unlit kitchen. He emptied his backpack on the granite counter top and pulled out several bottles—two of wine and two more of hard liquor. Caeleb added a couple boxes of beer to the mix. Glass twinkled against the counter, and it was followed by the sounds of cardboard game boxes, a slap of a stack of playing cards, and the racking of a gun.

In the corner of his eye, Orion saw Corvun and his friends stop moving.

Orion spun back around. He'd only ever heard that sound on old movies. Casper held a gun in his hand, pointed away from everyone and his finger off the trigger. He put the gun on the counter with a light *click*.

Ophiah shoved him hard. "Where did you get that?"

Something moved in Orion's peripheral vision again.

"It's dad's, okay?" Casper held his hands up in mock surrender. "Look, if we're gonna be here all weekend, *overnight*—" he raised his eyebrows, "—don't you think it's wise to have some sort of protection? I mean, this is exactly the kind of situation RUST would see as a field day."

Corvun slinked into Orion's sight, one hand out as if he was trying to comfort a distressed animal. But something about *Corvun* struck Orion as feral. Orion could feel Corvun's worry and unease like electricity standing the hairs on the back of his neck straight up. The way Corvun moved was calculated and stalking. Orion looked at him, and he noticed a blocky shape on his back underneath the folds of his tee.

Orion closed his eyes. Darkness threatened his vision. His balance wavered. *That's a gun, too.* He'd never seen a gun in person, and the sheer weight of the situation tied lead weights to his ankles. He knew he should've stayed home.

Which one would you rather hold the gun? A whisper in his ear. More followed. *The Son of Joy or the Son of Liberality? Knowledge is a weapon, knowledge is the weapon.*

Orion squeezed his eyes tighter shut, begging the voices to come back a different time. A clamor startled him. Orion turned again to find the blond boy stumbling over a coffee table.

Which son? Which son?

The blond shook his head, clasped his ears, then turned the corner and disappeared.

Orion furrowed his brow and took a step after him. The voices faded to background noise. All he could hear was his own thoughts, his own curiosity flaring like a sunrise, an epiphany. *Could he hear the voices too?*

"Are you out of your mind?" Ophiah cried again. "Why would you bring that here? You don't even know how to shoot it!"

"But I do," Corvun said slowly.

All eyes turned to him, Orion's included.

"My father taught me," Corvun said. He tilted his head to the side. "Did your daddy teach you, North?"

Casper's face burned red. "No," he said.

"Maybe I should hold onto it," Corvun offered.

"No," Casper said, firmer.

Corvun reeled back, stood up straighter. His figure took on authority—a kind Orion had never seen in Casper or the Canes brothers. In that moment, Orion knew if he had to pick a side for survival, it would be with Corvun.

The Son of Liberality, the Son of Liberality. The voices swirled in his head, circling in his mind. Another word, quieter, a name in a language he didn't understand. But he recognized it, as if he'd known it in a past life. The name was familiar, the name of a brother.

Orion excused himself in a crack of a voice and left. He followed in the blond kid's steps and found him sitting on the floor in the hall, staring with wide, pale eyes at the wall opposite him. Orion's legs seized up, and he sat a few feet off to the right of the boy's blank stare. Orion tried to place his name but couldn't come up with anything.

Do you know his name? Do you know? Do you know?

The boy's green eyes swung like spotlights and fixed on Orion's.

Orion felt the blood drain from his face, from his hands and feet. He looked away numbly. Orion had come to terms with his own truth. As the son of an angel and a demon, he could hear the whispers of spirits, good and bad. But what was the blond boy's truth? Did he know what he was hearing was the conversations of the supernatural? Did only the good haunt him, or did the bad plague him too? More importantly, did he know he wasn't the only one? Did he know he wasn't alone?

The confession danced on the tip of Orion's tongue.

VENATRIX CANES

The generator hummed to life. Venatrix stared in disbelief. The island had been abandoned for some time, but Cassie seemed to work miracles on anything with gears and motors. Venatrix rubbed the dirt from her hands onto her tight jeans. Beside her, Cassie dusted her hands off, too. Cassie wore grease-stained, baggy jeans with holes in the knees, a flattering spaghetti-strap top, and her hair undone and uncombed. Blond curls twisted everywhere, sticking to her neck and the sides of her mouth as she spoke.

"That should be good," Cassie said. Half-smiled. "You know, at least until a tree falls on it."

"What's the point of a backup generator for a hurricane party?" Venatrix asked.

"Cold beers?" Cassie lifted a half-empty, green bottle she'd snagged before they'd split from the group. Cassie's sticky fingers always amused Venatrix, especially her ability to steal from Venatrix's own brothers—who noticed everything.

"Aside from the booze," Venatrix said.

Cassie raised her eyebrows. "AC?"

Venatrix laughed.

. . . . .

Upstairs, Venatrix watched the party begin to bloom to life. Low, golden lights lit the room; backup lanterns and candles and pocket-sized lighters spotted the couch side tables and the coffee tables, the fireplace mantle and the dining table. The twenty-four packs of beers were open and cracked. Her brothers each held a bottle, and to her surprise, so did the Jude twins, Corvun, and his sister Cynthia. Her eyes locked on Corvun. He finished his can and immediately grabbed another.

She could read his thoughts straight from his expression: *I'm too sober for this.* Venatrix wondered what had gone down in the time she and Cassie had missed. She was about to approach him when Caeleb called her name. She hesitated, then walked to Caeleb.

Her brother handed her a beer. "Cheers." His glass clinked against hers.

Venatrix couldn't stop herself from looking back at Corvun.

"Well? Invite him to a game. Icebreaker," Caeleb decided. He shot Corvun a strange look—as if he couldn't tell if Corvun was still a brother or now an enemy. "Truth or dare or drink, to loosen us all up. Since it's been a while since he's talked to us." Caeleb gave a tight, strained smile. "His boyfriend can join, too."

Venatrix clenched her fists so she wouldn't shove Caeleb for the remark. Even though she knew very little about Corvun's new best friend, she hated Caeleb coming up with whatever reason he felt like best explained Corvun's behavior—or *anyone's* behavior for that matter. "Fine," she said. She left Caeleb there, craned over like a vulture, and felt his eyes follow her as she pulled Corvun aside.

Corvun's breath smelled like alcohol. His tired eyes brushed over the concern on her face.

"*Corvun,*" she whispered.

"*What?*" he whispered back.

"Is…" Venatrix looked around for Jayren.

"What?" Corvun pressed.

Venatrix bounced on her heels and wrung her hands. "Do… Do you want to play spin the bottle?"

"*What?*"

"You've said that three times now!" Venatrix snapped.

"What kind of *spin the bottle?* Is this some sick, twisted version your brothers came up with?" Corvun showed his teeth as he spoke.

"It's the truth or dare or drink version."

Corvun groaned. His accusing eyes surveyed the room, searching for Caeleb.

Venatrix stood in the way of her brother. "Please don't start anything."

"What's going on?" a voice hissed.

Venatrix jumped at the sharp voice. She looked up, and her body went numb. She twisted her fingers to feel something.

Jayren stood there. His eyes were dull and faded, rubbed red around the edges. He fixed a glare on her that made her feel much, much worse than any other glare she'd been subject to. "I thought you two weren't friends anymore."

"He's my best friend," she said before she could process the words leaving her mouth.

"He's *my* best friend," Jayren snapped back.

"Flattered," Corvun muttered.

"There's enough of him to share," Jayren mumbled. "Besides, you're kind of a shit friend if you ask me. Whatever happened to being dance partners? Study partners? It's like he doesn't exist to you anymore."

Venatrix's skin flamed. She reeled back, seething. Words tangled in her mouth.

"I'm right here," Corvun said.

Venatrix's mind snapped together into organized chaos, a feeling she was more than used to lately. Her world was turning upside down, and she was faced with this: the option to stand by her brothers or stand by her best friend and his new friends. She wasn't sure what to choose. "*Anyway*," she managed slowly, "I came to ask if you guys would want to play an icebreaker game."

Jayren looked to Corvun again.

Corvun looked at the floor. Then to Venatrix. "You know what they're tryin' to do, Vena," he said.

Venatrix wanted him to stop talking. She hated it—that it felt as if he could read her mind and put all her emotions on her sleeve for her. It was almost as if he knew her better than she knew herself. That alone made her want to cut some ties, if not all. Her emotions were a risk. He knew it; she knew it too. That's why he played them like a deck of cards. And Corvun *always* won at cards.

"They're tryin' to get you to pick a side," he leaned in, hissed in her ear. "Just promise me you pick wisely."

OPHIAH JUDE

Rain battered the window. Between flashes of lightning, the bowing palm trees could be seen through the storm. Wind rattled the shudders; the ocean crashed on the horizon.

Ophiah observed the group. They all sat together on the top floor, surrounded by several full-sized beds. A fleeting thought crossed her mind: Where would they all sleep? Anxiety coiled in her gut. She hoped Casper wouldn't ask her to sleep in the same bed. She promised herself if the topic came up, she would say that she and Orion agreed to share a bed. *To maintain purity,* she told herself.

If she was honest with herself, she could still feel where Casper's hands had been when they *were* together. His fingerprints burned her eternally, marred her like scars. *It was just once. It was a mistake.* If she could take it all back she would. If she could go back to the moment Casper asked her out, she would. She would've decided to be someone else. Strong. Solitary. But she'd allowed him to mold her into something weak and co-dependent. Love had turned her to rubble.

In the sloppy, cross-legged circle they made, whispers passed around, mutterings before someone took charge. Someone, who Ophiah knew would be Caeleb. Caeleb watched, too, meeting her eyes for just a moment to offer her a sly, knowing smile.

The quiet ones are the dangerous ones.

You are a dangerous one, dangerous one.

Across the circle, a pale blond boy shook his head. It was short and quick, a twitch, as if he was trying to shake off a bug. Orion noticed too, shifting beside her to whisper in her ear. "I think he hears them," Orion said, "the angels and the demons."

"Who is he?"

"I don't know, but he doesn't have a halo," Orion said.

"He's human?" Ophiah asked. She watched the boy closer. His skin shimmered in the moonlight, subtly, almost too dull to notice.

"I don't think so," Orion said.

Ophiah looked at the group under a new light. She'd grown up with a small knowledge of the angel hierarchy, but she knew enough. Her mother was an Archangel who walked the Earth as a human. All the Archangels walked together, broke bread together, knew each other as family. But there were only two couples among the Eight Archangels.

Valentine and Gabrielle North, and Samuel and Rachael Canes.

Cassie and Casper North; Caeleb and Erin and Venatrix Canes. They were the only children to hold the title of Archangel Heir. A rarity and an honor and risk to every move they made. They walked a fine line, some walked it worse than the others. But one thing they shared was a black-lined tattoo on the nape of their necks. Ophiah had seen Casper's once. It depicted a shield with four wings.

She'd heard rumors of the counterpart tattoos. A half-rank tattoo with a single pair of wings for the Nephilim children, sons or daughters with only one Archangel parent. That was where Corvun and Cynthia Khlyde fit. They were the children of Michael—which held weight in and of itself— and a saint. She'd heard the stories of their births because of the other Archangels' intervention. Corvun's mother had barely survived the delivery of her first son; the Archangels' prayers spared her. Her second pregnancy, however, killed her.

Still, Ophiah thought, *it's better than having a demon for a father.*

That was where she and Orion fit. Angelborne Halfbreeds. An invisible tattoo for their safety. Constant prayer to hide their existence from other demons. Valentine commanded the other angels to take the two of them into their protection. It was a small mercy, the time away from home and the abuse they endured there.

Ranks of Archangel Heir, Nephilim, and Halfbreed aside, there were few other categories the boy could fit into. Sentinels were known to have a halo, but like Orion had said, he didn't have one. Not that they could see, anyway. Ophiah watched the boy a while longer.

He looked around the room absently, fidgeting with his hands. He pushed his thick-rimmed glasses up the bridge of his nose. He made a point not to look at anyone, but his eyes slipped.

They fell on her, and she held them.

Ophiah smiled at him, small enough that Casper would write it off.

He didn't smile back. He paled, then turned red.

And his pupils narrowed for the briefest moment.

Ophiah leaned over to Orion. "Sentinel. Seaborne. He has to be," she whispered.

"What makes you say that?"

Ophiah hesitated.

Look at his eyes, look at his eyes. He has the eyes of an angel.

"Jayren," Corvun muttered.

The boy looked towards him.

Ophiah's attention drifted to Corvun, too. "Corvun's guardian," she speculated.

"He couldn't hurt a fly," Orion argued.

"Not yet," Ophiah said.

Orion furrowed his brow then shook his head, dismissing it.

Not yet, not yet, not yet.

Ophiah watched Jayren's features twist and grimace in time with the voices she heard.

ORION JUDE

In the corner of the room, the radio static flickered. Mutters continued around the circle, but Orion's focus was on Venatrix alone. She sat beside him in the circle, head down, a book in her lap. The longer he watched, he realized she wasn't reading it at all, or at least if she was, she wasn't reading very fast. She didn't flip any pages. Five minutes. Still nothing. Orion looked around to see if anyone else had noticed Venatrix's severe lack of interest in the book or company.

Finally, Erin cracked open a bottle of hard liquor.

Caeleb's eyes flashed eagerly, and he looked around the circle. "Truth or dare or drink," he announced. "Drinking is the opt-out."

"I'm *in*," Cynthia swooned. She earned a sharp glare from Corvun.

Three more girls and one older boy had joined the group since they'd sat down in the circle together—Krista, Mila, Shanvi, and Kadhi. Orion knew them mostly as friends of friends.

Krista was one of the more popular girls at their school. She was a tall brunette who always wore the latest trends and fur-and-suede boots. She had a pointed face and a high voice and called the shots in their friend group almost as much as Caeleb did. If Caeleb was the ringleader, Krista was his right-hand woman. Ophiah often hung out with her, too.

Mila was a small girl with curly black hair and wicked green eyes. She was soft spoken with a hoarse voice and wise words. Orion was convinced she was beyond her years—her grades passed everyone's, even Venatrix and Corvun, who kept top of class. Because the North Academy was closed to anyone but those aware of angelic and demonic presence on Earth, Orion had his guesses about Mila. He'd considered she might be a prophet, but he wasn't sure.

Shanvi was curled in the nook of Erin's arm. She was dark-skinned, dyed-blond, and beautiful by anyone's standards. Her long hair had black strands of her natural color, and her eyes were arctic blue chips. She was the introvert of their group, quiet. She didn't speak much, but she and Erin had a reputation of getting more wasted than the rest of them and disappearing into bathrooms or spare closets. Above her head, a flame flickered in the low light, the Mark of a Sentinel.

Kadhi was Cassie's boyfriend, and he wasn't in North Academy. In fact, he was older than all of them and worked directly for Valentine North—the founder of North Academy—at his medical institute. Kadhi had dark brown skin and black hair and shiny black eyes. His smile was infectious; no one could be around Kadhi without feeling the joy that radiated from him. Though, at the same time, Orion wondered if Kadhi would rat them out to Valentine North and if North would turn around and send out a rescue party to dismantle their hurricane party.

Caeleb put an empty beer bottle in the middle of the circle. "We'll start with spin the bottle. Then we'll go clockwise around the circle," he explained. He gave the bottle a spin. It landed on Kadhi. "Truth or dare."

"Or drink," Cynthia chipped in.

Kadhi's integrity seemed to get the best of him because he said, simply, "Truth."

"Does Professor North know about the party?" Caeleb asked. (It seemed Orion wasn't the only one worried about North.)

Kadhi exchanged glances with Cassie and Casper. "I haven't said a word to him."

"Incredible," Caeleb said with raised eyebrows. "Cassie, truth or dare or drink."

"Drink!" she said with an outstretched hand. She took a beer from Erin, who was passing out the drinks, and downed the bottle.

"Casper, you're up."

"Dare," Casper said.

"Propose to Ophiah," Erin yelled. A couple others gave some hoots.

Orion's skin bristled. To his surprise and horror, Casper *did* turn to Ophiah and took both of her hands in his.

"*Marry me,*" he said in earnest.

Ophiah laughed callously. "Ask in another five years."

Orion breathed a sigh of relief.

"Orion!"

Orion turned cold again. "What?"

"C'mon!"

"Truth," he said, wondering what damage it could really do. (He hated drinking.)

"Thoughts on our little sister?" Caeleb asked with a sinister smile. A trap.

Orion was suddenly very, very aware of Venatrix and where she sat right beside him. She shifted uncomfortably, hands flat on the ground as if she was getting ready to stand and leave. Orion swallowed the ball in his throat. "Smarter than both of you combined," he snapped.

Caeleb's face lit with astonishment. "Excuse me?"

Erin just laughed.

"You heard me," Orion said. He couldn't feel his body. Adrenaline pumped through him.

"Fine. Venatrix. Dare," her brother picked for her. He tipped his head. "Looks like we found you a match for your wits. Kiss him."

Venatrix stood in a fury. Orion expected her to cuss or maybe even kick him, but she didn't. She only walked away. Across the circle, Corvun rolled his eyes at Venatrix's outburst.

"Got something to say, Corvun?" Caeleb challenged.

"Yeah," Corvun said. "Maybe if you stopped tryin' to push boys on her she'd like you more."

Caeleb's nostrils flared, but he moved on to the next person in the circle. "Jayren. Truth or dare or drink," he said blandly.

"Uh," Jayren hesitated. A moment passed. "Dare?" his voice cracked as he spoke.

"Carry Vena's dare. Kiss someone."

Jayren turned beet red. "That's not how it's supposed to work."

Caeleb shrugged. "You can drink if you want."

Jayren's eyes widened. He leaned over to Cynthia, who sat beside him, and kissed her cheek quickly. His face turned an undiscovered shade of red, and he stared at his hands in his lap.

Cynthia beamed. "Drink," she said. Caeleb chuckled and tossed her a beer can. Cynthia shotgunned the beer, and Corvun covered his face. Before Caeleb could call on Corvun, Corvun stood and left the circle, too.

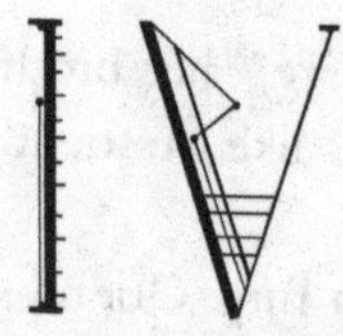

CORVUN KHLYDE

Corvun found Venatrix on the deck outside. Wind and rain ripped through her hair, soaking it into swinging, black tendrils. He shielded his face as he ventured out into the storm. "Vena! Come back inside!" he shouted.

Venatrix shook her head.

You would think it was a clear night sky, Corvun thought bitterly.

Lightning struck in the distance, and Corvun lunged forward into the storm and grabbed Venatrix's shoulders. He turned her around, fixed her with a firm glare (returned by an equally cold one), then dragged her back inside. She shouted at him as soon as they were back in the house.

"Leave me alone!"

"Are you tryin' to get yourself killed?" he yelled. "I get it! Your brothers are morons, but you don't have to go off and do somethin' stupid every time they say somethin' you don't like."

"They don't just *say* stuff, Corvun," she argued. She dripped on the oriental rug beneath her bare feet. Her eyes were as bright as lightning, a telltale sign of her heritage. "They make me do it! They made me come here!"

"What?" Corvun breathed.

"The power of influence the Archangels have, Corvun, we have it too."

Corvun paused. He knew about the ability. His father had it. The Eight Archangels embodied the Eight Virtues—kindness, abstinence, chastity, diligence, patience, liberality, humility, and joy. Their power of influence was used typically only to encourage humans in the right direction, to follow those virtues. Corvun had no idea the power could be used against other angels—nonetheless for something as crude as partying, drugs, or alcohol.

Venatrix faltered with her words, "It—it's... They're not strong enough...on their own. Just one of them can't do it. Caeleb can't force me to do anything. Erin can't either. But if they're both in on it..."

Corvun exhaled. *That changes things,* he thought. It also meant she didn't want to be here—not really. It all made sense—Caeleb and Erin and their posse. Corvun couldn't believe anyone in their right mind stuck around with her brothers. Corvun took a step forward, arm outstretched, as if Venatrix would run if he moved too fast. These days, he wouldn't be surprised. "I can tell Michael—"

"No!" she blurted. "Do you know what they'll do?"

"Not if your parents—"

"Corvun, you're not *listening.* They won't *stop.*"

Corvun held his tongue.

"Even if you did convince Michael and my parents... What would they do? Put them in juvie? They have no grounds. Besides, after whatever punishment they'd get, they'd just turn around and take it out on me."

Corvun was speechless for a moment. "What—what about Marks?"

"Are you kidding?" Venatrix narrowed her eyes, her lips pulled in hysterics. "Archangels don't *Mark* each other."

"They have," Corvun said. Then again, quieter, "*They have.* The Jude twins are Marked for their protection. Why wouldn't they do it to protect you?"

Glass shattered downstairs, followed by a flash of light and a bellowing crash of thunder.

"Did you hear that?" Venatrix whispered.

Numbly, Corvun nodded.

Together, they rushed inside.

Corvun listened to his and Venatrix's heels pound down the grand staircase that led downstairs. He could barely hear them, barely hear the thundering storm outside, over the numbing kick of his heart. When they reached the foyer, Corvun reached around his back and felt for the handle of his father's gun. "Where do you think it came from?" he whispered to Venatrix.

She was shaking. "I-I don't know…"

Another crash sounded, almost directly in time with a roar of thunder, off to their right.

"The kitchen," Venatrix whispered.

"Stay behind me," Corvun whispered back. He crept towards the kitchen. The gun quaked in his hand. He gripped it harder. Straight ahead of them, the curio cabinets were filled with silver and gold trimmed plates that flashed in the wild lightning from outside. Something else flashed, too. A warm flicker of light as a silhouette darted out of sight. Corvun pushed Venatrix into the open pantry beside them.

Thunder bellowed overhead, and the house shook and rattled around them. Glass spice jars shivered in the pantry door as Venatrix swung it shut, cowering inside.

"Show yourself!" Corvun yelled.

"D-Don't shoot! Don't shoot!" a familiar voice yelled. The silhouette came back into sight, standing against the bright windows with his hands in the air. Lightning struck behind Corvun, illuminating the face of his long time friend and his wide, chestnut eyes. A halo burned above his head.

"Josh?" Corvun yelled in disbelief. "You've got to be kiddin' me! You scared us shitless!"

"You?" Joshuah yelled back. "I'm the one at gunpoint!"

Corvun lowered the gun. "Why are you here?" he demanded.

Joshuah exhaled through thinned lips. "You're in danger."

The words tingled on his skin like ice, rose the hairs on the back of his neck. It was a Sentinel's gift to sense danger, and because they both knew that Joshuah was Corvun's guardian angel, Corvun couldn't argue the fact. "You could've just *texted*," Corvun hissed.

"You know that's not how this works, Corv," Joshuah said.

The pantry door squeaked.

Corvun looked over his shoulder.

Venatrix peered around the corner of the door. "Josh!" she gasped. She sidestepped the door and ran to him, throwing her arms around his middle.

Corvun followed her closely, grabbed Joshuah's arm as soon as Venatrix released him, and dragged him back to the staircase. "What do you mean we're in danger?" Corvun demanded quietly. "Is it the storm, or is it…"

Joshuah held his gaze. "It's not the storm. Someone else is here," he whispered.

"Where?" Corvun lowered his voice, leaned closer.

"I don't know."

Corvun looked back to Venatrix. "We have to warn the others."

JAYREN OMANS

Not yet, not yet, not yet, not yet… Voices twirled in Jayren's mind. He still felt Cynthia's cheek on his lips and the blush she left on his face in return. His stomach was somersaulting endlessly; he felt that the house might tip upside down at any given moment. In the corner of the room, the radio snapped and crackled and announced that Helix had reached a category three, just one hour before landfall was expected.

"The last direct hit the Northeast corner was Hurricane Kyle back in 2032," the reporter said. *"The storm followed World War III, and because of the damage done, the expense of rebuilding, and the uprise of RUST at that time, most families chose to move into the Jacksonville area. Helix is expected to cause even more, lasting damage to the area, perhaps causing the remaining population to follow in the tracks of those before them."*

The house creaked around the meager party, the whispers and rumors. Erin and Shanvi were sitting against the foot of the couch, locking lips and tongues. Cynthia was drunk beside Jayren, swapping dirty jokes with Caeleb—who found the younger girl amusing.

But Jayren couldn't focus.

A girl whispered off to his right. "Not yet," urgency laced her words.

Jayren's eyes snapped to her. It was the girl who'd smiled at him earlier, and as far as Jayren was concerned, she was drop-dead gorgeous. He was sure there wasn't a single girl who could top her looks. Ophiah's evergreen eyes locked with his again. A pretty blush dusted her freckles rose-petal pink. A strand of crimson hair fell in her face and she tucked it behind her ear. A delicate diamond twinkled there.

Something about *her* struck him as different. It was like her eyes were portals, like puddles as still as glass, that reflected straight back into his. Her pain was palpable like his, as if he could reach out and touch her fingertips and feel a frequency that burned in his body too.

Orion spoke beside her, and she looked away.

A lump formed in Jayren's throat.

Not yet, not yet. Wait until they sleep.

Both of the red-head twins stopped moving.

Jayren's hands turned cold. Were they hearing the same things? He'd had the same sickening feeling when Orion sat with him in the hallway. He had to find Corvun. He figured between Corvun and Venatrix and the crazy conspiracy theories they believed about angels and demons, they'd have an answer for him. Jayren stood, then stopped again.

That meant he'd have to *tell* Corvun about the voices.

And every time he'd told someone in the past, he'd be cut off and referred to a mental hospital.

Wait until they sleep, then you can leave the closet.

Ophiah grabbed Orion's wrist. "Ri, did you hear that?"

To Jayren's horror, Orion looked up at Jayren. "Where are you going?" Orion asked him.

Jayren opened his mouth to speak. His voice failed on the first syllable. "I—uh, I'm gonna go look for Corvun. He's been gone for a while, and I'm…"

"Worried?" Orion asked, lowering his voice.

Jayren nodded. He was worried about a lot of things currently. One of them was the fact that Orion and Ophiah were both standing up and approaching him. He couldn't figure out where to look to make things less awkward so he settled for looking at their shoes. "He was looking for Vena, and he's not back yet—"

Ophiah side stepped the both of them and headed for the stairs. "We have to check all the closets," she said as she jogged down the stairs. Orion and Jayren followed close on her heels. "If there's someone here, they could be dangerous."

Orion grabbed Ophiah's shoulders at the bottom of the stairs and spun her around. "*We* can't check the closets. It has to be Corvun or Casper," he said.

"Why?"

"Because they have *guns*," Orion whispered. "You know RUST assassins are always armed. We wouldn't stand a chance. It would be a bloodbath!"

"Better dead then stuck in a dead-end relationship," Ophiah snapped. She pulled away.

Jayren widened his eyes and stared after her. "Is she talking about you?"

"No. She's talking about her relationship with her boyfriend, Casper," Orion said. "It's an arranged courtship."

Jayren's eyes widened more. "Dude, those have been outdated since the 1700s."

"Not with us," Orion mumbled. He followed Ophiah.

Not with us? Jayren watched them walk down the dark hall. He wondered what it meant. He guessed that they may be into the same stuff Corvun was, and even with what little Jayren knew about the angel theories, he wouldn't be surprised if arranged courtships were on the table.

VENATRIX CANES

Venatrix's nerves were electric. Every swaying shadow made her jump in her skin, made her pulse bleed fire. Corvun and Joshuah breathed quietly behind her as she led them back through the house. A silhouette moved on the staircase, and Venatrix put her hand out, stopping Corvun with an arm across his chest.

"Ow! Stop stepping on my toes! Just go!" a girl whispered urgently.

"Wait," Venatrix uttered.

"Do you smell them?" a boy asked.

"What do you mean *do I smell them?*" a nasally voice returned.

"That's Jayren," Corvun said.

Three figures clambered down the stairs.

"Shhhh!" Corvun urged.

"Well, I wouldn't have fallen if he didn't push me!" Jayren waved a finger at Orion.

Orion spoke in a hushed voice. "I didn't push you! I was trying to see if you got closer maybe *then* you could smell who it was!"

"Dude, he's killing me," Jayren said, looking to Corvun, exasperated. "He thinks I can smell you."

Venatrix glanced at Corvun. "Only Sentinels can do that." Her eyes wandered to Joshuah.

Joshuah and Corvun both squinted at Jayren. Joshuah leaned closer. Lightning flashed, and realization dawned on Joshuah's face. "Seaborne," he said. "His skin is reflective under holy light."

Venatrix glanced at the window. Her stomach twisted; she hadn't even thought of it that way. Storms *were* often holy battles waged between angels and demons in the skies above. Had that have been the first thought when her brothers said "hurricane party" she might've fought harder against it or at least warned her parents about the plans.

"That's what we thought," Orion said. "We just can't see his halo."

"Corvun, man, what are they talking about? I'm not an angel, and I don't have a halo. God, you'd think I'm auditioning for some sort of bad-boy rom-com."

"He has a halo," Joshuah said to Corvun. "It's insanely hard to see, but it's there."

"He doesn't buy into it," Corvun said back, "the angels and demons and the Bible."

"Yeah, that's because it's a two-thousand year old book written by dudes tripping on beaches. Come on, this stuff isn't really *real*." Jayren looked around at the five surrounding him. His face was pale in the storm light, and something about his expression was conflicted. Doubting. He was doubting.

Maybe he does believe, Venatrix thought. *Maybe he just doesn't want to.*

"Corv, can I talk to you?" Jayren whispered, then lowered his voice more. "Alone?"

Corvun stepped away from Venatrix, and she watched the two disappear into the living room.

JAYREN OMANS

Jayren wrung his hands as he stepped into the circle of furniture. He felt as if he was standing in an amphitheater, full of people. It was as if everything he said here would be carried to the twins, to the other kids in the house, that his secrets would betray him. Social suicide. That's what it felt like.

He faced Corvun.

Corvun stood there like a pillar, steady, unwavering, everlasting. Something about him made Jayren feel a little more okay with sharing his secret. Maybe Corvun already knew.

Jayren closed his eyes and exhaled carefully. His throat squeezed. "I want to tell you something," he said under his breath. "Do you promise you'll still be my friend?"

Corvun didn't respond.

Jayren opened his eyes.

Corvun was staring at him, pale. "Why wouldn't I be your friend?"

Jayren's brow pinched. Heat welled in his eyes. "Because every other person I've *told* ends up deciding not to be my friend anymore."

"I promise," Corvun whispered, hoarse. His eyes held secrets, too, Jayren could tell. He'd seen that look in the mirror all of his life.

"I hear voices." The words were barely audible. He closed his eyes, and the tears wiggled loose. "I've always heard them. Sometimes they just repeat other people. Sometimes they taunt me. Sometimes they tell me to do awful things. Sometimes it feels like there's someone whispering in my ear."

"Will you come sit down?" Corvun asked weakly.

Jayren nodded. His legs felt like noodles as he crossed the room to sit on the covered couch beside Corvun. His armpits were damp, and his neck was hot. He wanted to run outside, straight into the storm, down the road, and as far as his legs would carry him.

"Jayren, they're right," Corvun whispered. "You're a Sentinel. The voices you hear… They're angels and demons."

Jayren stood. Fire consumed his body. "Is this a joke? Do you think it's funny?"

"Jayren, please sit down."

He sat stiffly.

"I believe you. Joshuah…" Corvun motioned to the hall "He's a Sentinel, too. He showed up because there's someone else here in the house with us. He's my guardian angel. He came because I'm—because *we're* in danger." He met Jayren's eyes; his eyes were heavy and black. "The voices you're hearin'—they're spirits in the house. They know things, too. That's what you hear. They talk to each other."

Somehow, hearing Corvun explain his strange twist on things was an easier pill to swallow than a cold shoulder. Jayren sat and kept listening numbly. He tried to wrap his head around it and really believe it; part of him already *did* believe it, like a sixth sense. There was something not quite right about the twin's syncopation and Venatrix's glowing eyes. But he really, really hated to believe any of it. If he faced it, believed it, that meant he'd have to believe God hated him enough to let his father kill himself and his mother go mentally insane.

The tears kept coming.

"Are you okay?" Corvun asked. "What's wrong? Shouldn't that—shouldn't you…"

"Shouldn't I what?" Jayren snapped, sharper than he wanted to.

Corvun hesitated. "Feel better? Now that you know?"

Jayren just shook his head.

Corvun sat very still then, slowly, wrapped an arm around Jayren's shoulders.

Jayren dropped his head in Corvun's neck and let the tears go. He figured that if there really was someone in the house with them—if all of the conspiracies were true—they were all about to die and that likely meant he was about to head straight to Hell. It seemed like a good enough reason to cry to him.

Jayren wasn't sure how long he sat there, but it was long enough to make his bones stiff and his muscles ache. When the crick in his neck was too much to bear, he sat up and sniffled.

"Jayren," Corvun said carefully. He sounded younger than he was, just a child. "What were the voices sayin'?"

Jayren swallowed at the knot in his throat, swiped at the snot on his upper lip. Then he whispered, "Wait until they sleep."

ORION JUDE

Orion sat on the stairs beside his twin, staring at where Venatrix sat on the bottom step. Her head was turned to the spot where Corvun and Jayren disappeared twenty minutes earlier. Every now and then she glanced back to the mouth of the hall where Joshuah stood with alert eyes and a tense posture. She fidgeted with her hands and the ends of her hair. Orion wondered if her fingertips were cold.

"Ten bucks," Ophiah whispered.

Orion gritted his teeth. "You're wrong about her," he whispered back. He stood and walked down the stairs until he was right beside Venatrix.

The pale girl looked up at him. Her irises were storm blue with flickers of electricity shining in the centers. Orion already knew about the power in her family, the power that flowed directly in her blood, too. He thought momentarily that he should be afraid of her. But against his better senses, he sat beside her.

"Hi," he said.

"Hi," she said.

"I'm—"

"Orion Jude," she said. "I know who you are."

"I guess that's a given in our school." Orion gave a small, forced laughed. Then, quietly, "Venatrix."

She smiled lightly. A rosy blush dusted the sides of her face. "You've hung out with my brothers a lot lately."

"Yeah. But it's not—it's not what you think." Orion rubbed his neck, embarrassment simmering.

Venatrix perched her chin in her palm. "Then what is it?"

"My sister—Ophi—she's dating Casper North. Casper's friends with them. It's just a mutual friend group I guess. I don't know, I wish I could make other friends." He watched her eyes dance over his face.

"Are you hitting on me?" she asked.

Orion shook his head fervently, lips pressed tight. "I just thought—maybe we could be friends. You don't seem like you like your brothers. I don't like your brothers. The enemy of my enemy is my friend, you know?"

The corner of Venatrix's lips pointed upwards in a tiny, quirky smile.

Orion opened his mouth to say something else, maybe try to find their common interests, but Venatrix's eyes focused on something behind him. Orion turned to see Corvun and Jayren emerge from the living room. Corvun looked as if he'd died and come back to life; Jayren's skin and eyes were flushed red with emotion.

"Let's go upstairs," Corvun said, loud enough to make Orion look around anxiously. "We haven't even broke out the weed yet, and I'm ready to crash."

Venatrix sat up straighter.

Jayren looked like he was about to hurl.

And Orion knew exactly why.

The voices returned, curling in Orion's ears.

Wait until they sleep, then you can leave the closet.

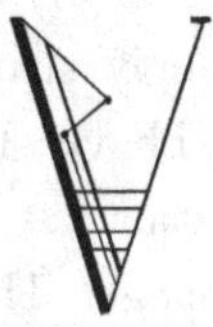

ORION JUDE

The six of them retreated upstairs. No one spoke a word.

As the night grew darker, the storm grew louder. Wind creaked against the house, occasionally snapping siding off. Trees shuddered; waves roared and groaned. The sky trembled with thunder, and lightning cut clean across the horizon, threatening to slice into the meagerly boarded windows.

Everyone else had already retired—either too high or too drunk to do anything but lay immobile in the teeth of the storm.

Orion quivered in the bed he shared with Ophiah. He looked straight ahead, over the edge of their bed. On the floor between his and the next, Corvun and Jayren and Joshuah laid on thin, blue sleeping bags. In the next bed over, Venatrix clutched the edge of her cover and stared into space with wide, worried eyes. Orion watched her until her eyes snapped to his.

"Stop looking at me," she whispered. "I can feel you looking at me."

"Sorry," Orion said. He stared at her white hands on the covers instead.

"You're still looking at me."

Orion squeezed his eyes shut. "Sorry!" Instead, he listened to Corvun and Jayren talk to each other.

"How can I hear angels and demons?" Jayren asked.

Corvun sighed, seemingly struggling to find the right words. "I'm not really sure. I have a book I can loan you about it, though. I think it's because as a guardian angel, you're meant to be able to sense danger. The spirits here on Earth—good and bad—they can see more than we see, sort of like an omniscient eye. Make sense?"

"No," Jayren said.

"Okay," Corvun said.

"Have you ever watched a show in a different language?" Joshuah spoke up.

Jayren's head shuffled against his sleeping bag.

"Ever thought you could almost understand them? Without subtitles?"

Jayren didn't move.

Joshuah continued, "Sentinels have the Gift of Tongues. We're able to understand anyone—any language, any dialect—that way we can help them if they're in trouble or danger. The Gift of Tongues also allows us to hear and understand spirits when they speak." A pause. "The spirits always speak, but only Sentinels can understand them."

"I can hear them, too," Orion whispered.

Joshuah turned his head. "Are you a Sentinel? I can't see your halo."

Orion shook his head, but it was Corvun who spoke. "He's Angelborne," Corvun said quietly. Then even quieter, as if he didn't want to say it at all, "A Halfbreed."

"I see," Joshuah said.

Orion hated the way their voices sounded when they said it, like the words were poison in their mouths.

"You hear them because demons hear them," Venatrix said. Her tone of voice was different. Resolute. "You have demon blood. It only makes sense that you could hear the spirits, too."

Orion looked at her again. She held no prejudice in her eyes, no disdain. It was different than the way the other Archangels looked at him. Different, even, than how Corvun looked at him.

Wind whistled and howled outside, but the sound grew fainter as their stakeout dragged on.

OPHIAH JUDE

The storm was quiet as the eye passed over the house. In the corner of the room, the radio flickered and stuttered, warning people not to leave their homes, despite the temporary calm. Ophiah stirred in her bed. In the absence of the hurricane, the whispers were faint at first, just a coil of mist on the air. Then they picked up, rushing, like a stream of water. All at once.

She's coming. She's coming. She's coming.

She followed suit. "She's coming," she whispered.

Beside her, her brother turned stone-still. The others quit talking.

Silence spread over them like an evening shadow. No one said a word, and the time stretched too.

"Corvun, what do we do?" Venatrix murmured.

Corvun didn't reply.

Joshuah breathed deep. "I'll go scope the scene."

"I'm goin' with you," Corvun said quickly, quietly. "The rest of you stay here."

No one objected; Ophiah guessed the others didn't need to be told. She, on the other hand, felt forces out of her control beckoning her to follow the two boys as they stood, flattened their clothes, as Corvun picked up the black pistol and held it in a vice-like grip. She watched them walk out the door at the far, west end of the bedroom.

Time turned to quicksand, dragging and lethargic. Ophiah felt her limbs go numb waiting. The voices danced around her head, but now they spoke nonsense. *Maybe,* she thought, *they're speaking a language I don't understand. Words I don't know, in an angelic tongue.* That's what the voices spoke the most—angelic or demonic tongues. She understood both, but she understood the demonic tongues like a first language.

A number flashed across her vision, too quick to register. Numbers, she understood.

She more than understood.

She'd seen it before during travel. A car would pass, and a date would rip through the forefront of her mind. She'd later see the car upside down, in flames, or crumpled like a piece of paper.

Numbers were a universal, sure sign of death.

She pushed the covers off her legs.

"What are you doing?" Orion snapped.

"I'm going with them," Ophiah whispered back.

Orion turned and grabbed her arm before she could stand. "It's *dangerous.*"

"I know." She yanked her wrist free. As soon as she lost contact with her twin, she felt the anxiety set in. She knew Orion wouldn't follow her; he wasn't the bold one. Something in *her* craved destruction and chaos, and she'd follow that calling to any end. She tip-toed across the bedroom, lifted a wary hand to the white-wooden door, and pushed. The black hall gaped back at her.

Ophiah ventured slowly down the steps, careful to wait and listen at every turn. The carpet pressed softly beneath her bare feet. When she reached the kitchen they'd been in earlier, she peered around for anything she could use as a weapon. One bottle of wine was left, unopened, on the granite countertop. Ophiah crept forward and grabbed the neck of the bottle with a fist.

CORVUN KHLYDE

Corvun and Joshuah walked back-to-back. The unusual feeling of Joshuah's shoulders against his made Corvun even more aware of each of his senses. He smelled the damp rain outside and the saturated earth around the house. He heard the bristling of the palm trees in the weakened winds, the distant roar of the storm all around them. His hands were sweaty on the hilt of the nine-millimeter in his hand. The green night-sights poked holes in his eyes. He carried the gun level with the average man's chest. Finger on the trigger.

Never put your finger on the trigger until you have eyes on your target, Michael's voice warned in his head.

But Corvun knew how the RUST assassins moved.

"Watch," Michael instructed. He lifted a small, black piece of sticky-tack. He watched Corvun's eyes as Corvun followed the sticky-tack into a slingshot. Michael pulled back. "This movement is important." He moved the slingshot loose again. "They start here. Then they pull back." Michael pulled the slingshot back again. "Then they release."

Michael let go of the sticky-tack, and it catapulted across the room in a heartbeat. It stuck against the wall.

Corvun tried to understand.

"It won't be easy to learn. It's even harder to fight. Their center of gravity is where you aim, but the rest of their bodies will be a mist, like shadows."

Corvun nodded, his focus unwavering.

"Again," Michael said. "This time, try to catch it."

It took three months before Corvun could knock his father's sticky-tack from mid-air.

Every time the shadows moved, Corvun jumped. Palm trees scratched against the windows, sending shivers down Corvun's neck. "Do you see anyone?" he breathed to Joshuah.

"No," Joshuah whispered. He gripped the largest kitchen knife they could find in his hand. "Corvun, I don't think this is a good idea."

Black fluttered past Corvun's vision.

It froze his pulse, then sent it into a flurry. Corvun held his breath, eyes wide. He looked around. "She's here."

"You know we don't stand a chance," Joshuah said. His voice cracked.

Metal clattered across the entry way floor.

"Corvun!" Joshuah yelled.

Corvun swiveled. In the dark, he could barely see the flash of steel on the tile floor. Out of Joshuah's hand. Someone had disarmed him. Corvun held his father's gun tighter. His fingers were going numb. He twisted again, trying to spot anything in the low, storm light. "Get behind me," Corvun ordered.

A figure moved in his periphery.

He spun.

Gone.

Corvun's heart thundered in his ears. His throat squeezed.

The knife scraped against the floor.

Turn.

The knife was gone.

"Corvun," Joshuah pressed again. "*Look.*" He pointed at the living room.

The figure sat, legs crossed, on the arm of a sheet-covered chair. The silhouette was feminine, and the knife glinted in her hands as she twisted it. "Do you know the bounty on your head, Fames?" she asked in a sly, low voice.

Joshuah tried to step in front of Corvun, but Corvun shoved him away, irritated. He leveled the gun at the figure. His finger pulled back. Too slow.

The gun fired off, three times.

Pack, pack, pack.

Into the ceiling.

A leather-clad hand held Corvun's arm above his head.

The other hand plunged the knife into his gut.

Corvun sucked in a tight breath. His lungs contracted. His muscles contracted against the foreign object in his body, the splitting pain that burned his stomach. His vision went white with pain. He squeezed his eyes shut. The gun fell from his hand. He doubled over.

Something shattered.

Liquid sprayed him.

Red. Dripping.

The assassin fell.

In front of Corvun, Ophiah stood with a broken bottle. She dropped the daggered glass when she saw Corvun's hand at his stomach. He broke her horrified gaze, fumbled one-handed for the pistol on the floor. Bending over cut his insides with a hot, searing pain. He grabbed the handle and emptied the rest of the magazine into the unconscious assassin. Four ear-splitting bangs.

Then heaviness fell over him.

The heaviness of the gun.

The heaviness of the blood seeping across the floor.

Heaviness of his eyelids, of his body collapsing.

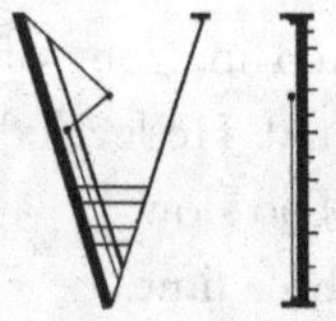

CORVUN KHLYDE

Hospital lights flashed overhead. One. Two. Three. Four. Metal wheels squeaked against linoleum floors. Murmurs. A steady beeping. Cool drugs in his veins.

Then heaviness.

Darkness returned.

VENATRIX CANES

Venatrix sat in the hospital waiting room with Jayren, Orion, and Ophiah. None of the others attending the hurricane party had been allowed into the waiting room. They'd been ushered off alarmingly fast by the other Archangels. Only Valentine and Gabrielle and Michael stayed behind. They stood in different spots in the waiting room with Venatrix and her classmates. Michael stood watching the door. Valentine stood at the window, glaring out into the hazy horizon. Gabrielle was at his side with a hand on his arm. Her lips moved swiftly.

The silver double doors opened, and a fourth Archangel stepped out. He had snow-white hair and crystal blue eyes. He glanced at Michael over thin-rimmed glasses. "Your son will be fine," Doctor Bennett said. "He's awake and resting."

Venatrix's heart raced. She looked between the doctor and Michael, hoping she could see Corvun soon.

Michael's militaristic figure relaxed. His shoulders gave, his expression softened. His dark brows and black eyes took in the doctor; he walked forward to embrace the doctor like a brother. Venatrix had heard Corvun complain many, many times about his father's brutal training regimes, but it was clear to her at least that Michael still cared for his son in his own way. Venatrix was still watching when the two pulled away from each other. Michael turned to her. She looked at Valentine only to find him and his wife looking at the four of them, too. Venatrix shifted in her seat.

Valentine and Michael exchanged a glance.

MICHAEL KHLYDE

Valentine held the door for Michael. Michael stepped into the private room, finding a place against the wall to stand and face his friend. Valentine closed the door. It clicked quietly, and Valentine rubbed his face. The close smell of latex gloves and sanitizer and tissue filled the hollow space between them. The blue-gray walls closed in. "We'll have to alter their memories."

Michael said nothing. He'd known this verdict was coming. In fact, the other children were already undergoing selective memory alteration as they spoke. The party should've never happened, but all Eight of them had been on the Mediating Grounds and in the line of defense in one of the many unseen wars they fought. *How ironic*, he thought. *The war I should've been fightin' was right under my nose.*

Valentine pulled a chair and sat. Sunkissed locks of his hair fell into his face. He massaged the scruff on his dark skin.

Michael sat opposite of him. "How did we let this happen?" he asked.

Valentine shook his head and hung it a moment later. "We have to keep a closer eye on them. They're in danger, brother. It's clear they'll find one another, but it's too soon."

Michael paused, pondered these things. The five children—Venatrix, Jayren, Orion, Ophiah, and his own son—their inevitable gravity pulled each other into a dangerous orbit. It dragged a great responsibility with it and an even greater risk.

"If they continue like this—Michael—what if they fall?" Valentine looked up and a broken expression riddled his face. "They're so young. They could get so turned around, so quickly."

"How much longer?" Michael asked. *How much longer until they form that unbreakable bond of kinship? How much longer before we can stop their callin'? How much longer can we protect them?* There weren't enough words to capture the worry he held.

"As long as we can," Valentine said. "Your son—he still has two years before he'll be inducted to RUST. Two years."

"What if it's the wrong thing to do?" Michael pressed. "What if they *need* each other?"

"I believe they'll find each other again. But this," Valentine said, spreading his hands open before him, "it's something they shouldn't have to carry with them."

The party.

The paranoia.

An encounter with RUST.

An encounter with an assassin.

Death.

"We carried things much like that," Michael said, looking Valentine in the eye. He held the gaze. He remembered, too—the first lives they took when they'd been partners in RUST, the blood, the destruction and chaos they'd caused.

"They're still so young," Valentine said. "Two years."

Michael closed his eyes. He nodded. "Two years, on one condition."

Valentine waited.

"Corvun keeps his memories. The others—they only remember a normal party."

Valentine nodded.

Michael sighed and stood. He stepped towards the door. One hand on the door, and Valentine spoke up once more.

"Do you think *that's* the right thing to do?"

Michael paused. He'd always sworn God had carved it out of his bones to lie, so he said, "I don't know."

CORVUN KHLYDE

Corvun walked into North Academy. Golden sunlight trickled in through high-set skylights. The plated lockers shimmered in the light, and as students opened and closed the lockers, flashes of light blinded him. It seemed too serene, too calm, too *safe*.

He stood for a moment, not knowing where to go. He wondered if his classmates remembered *anything*. His father had given him a quick, emotionless debrief on the topic. Venatrix and Jayren—they would know the party happened, but if Corvun mentioned anything about the RUST assassin that attacked them, they wouldn't remember.

But he remembered all of it. He had the scar to prove it, too, temporary as it might be.

A heavy loneliness settled over him, and it reminded him even more of that night. He wondered if he could try to probe memories out of Venatrix and Jayren, hint at games they played or conversations they had. Corvun thought harder, only to realize the party was the first time the two had met. He wondered if they'd ever be friends again, and it carved a trench in his heart.

Jayren appeared in Corvun's peripheral vision. He skidded up, bouncing with energy. "Dude—did you hear? You should hear what happened at the party! Okay, so you know how you and I were downstairs? Well, *upstairs*—"

Corvun found comfort in Jayren's high-pitched voice. He settled into a slow stride beside Jayren and let Jayren override his memories of the hurricane party with the new stories of the last party he'd ever go to.

Corvun glanced upward in the direction they headed, and for the briefest moment, his sights lock with Venatrix's eyes. She surveyed him warily, offered him the smallest twitch of a smile.

It made him wonder.

ACKNOWLEDGMENTS

Since this story is short and sweet, I'll keep the acknowledgments the same.

Thank you to my Lord and Savior, Jesus Christ. For everything. These characters have healed me in ways that I will never be able to put into words.

Thank you to my readers. Thank you to those of you who continue to show up at my booths and ask about new releases or rave about those that you've read. I never expected my books to find places in the hearts of others.

It's the honor of a lifetime. Thank you.

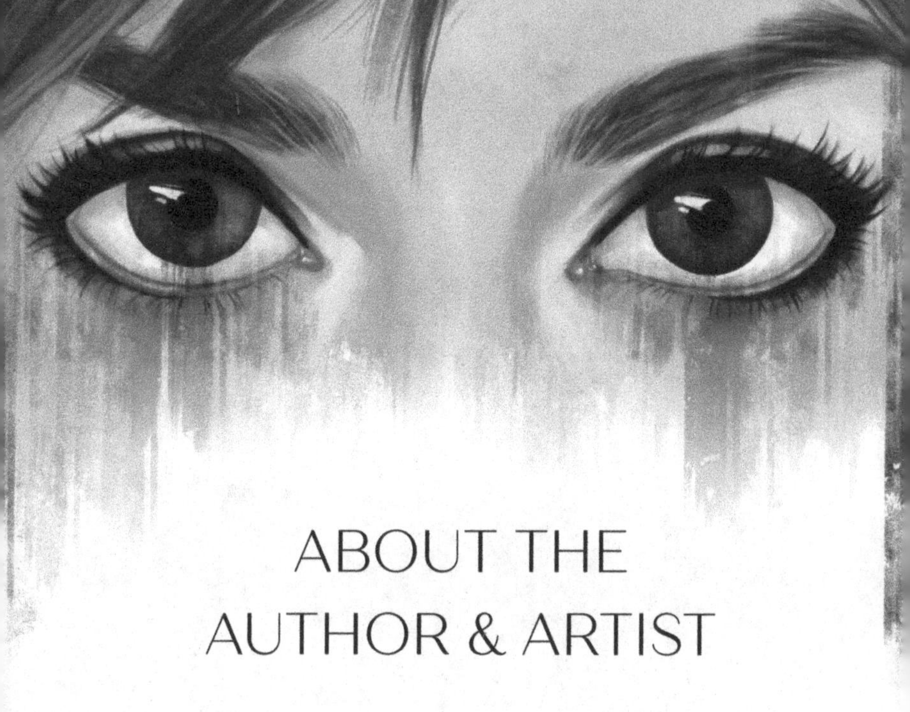

ABOUT THE AUTHOR & ARTIST

R. D. G. Lover is an artist, author, and freelancer. She owns a small business where she sells her original art and takes freelance work for editing services, website design, graphic design, custom paintings, and more. Lover spends her free time stargazing, singing loudly in her car, and working on her illustrated novels about the Four Horsemen of the Apocalypse. She has made it her goal to write and illustrate a novel in every genre.

Her website, www.4pocalypseArts.com, showcases a gallery of all-original art and writing from her stories. To stay up to date with R. D. G. Lover's future releases, be sure to subscribe to her newsletter on her website and follow her on any social media @4pocalypseArts.

9 781972 005019